THE BLAST OFF KID

by Laura Driscoll
Illustrated by Rebecca Thornburgh

The Kane Press
New York

Book Design/Art Direction: Roberta Pressel

Library of Congress Cataloging-in-Publication Data

Driscoll, Laura.
    The Blast Off Kid/by Laura Driscoll; illustrated by Rebecca Thornburgh.
        p. cm. — (Math matters.)
    Summary: For a chance to win a trip to Space Camp, James sets out to collect 10,000 Blast Off Energy Bar wrappers, grouping them as he goes to make counting easier, and soon the whole town is helping him out..
        ISBN 1-57565-130-0 (alk. paper)
        [1. Contests—Fiction. 2. Counting—Fiction.] I. Thornburgh, Rebecca McKillip, ill. II. Title. III. Series.
    PZ7.D79BI 2003
    [E]—dc21
    2002156221

10 9 8 7 6 5 4 3 2 1

First published in the United States of America in 2003 by The Kane Press.
Printed in Hong Kong.

MATH MATTERS® is a registered trademark of The Kane Press.

Every day Jim brought his lunch to school.
And every day, it was the same—a sandwich,
an apple, and a Blast Off Energy Bar.
   Jim *loved* Blast Off Bars.

Jim's friends Everett and Rachel liked Blast Off Bars, too. But not the way Jim did. He had tried every single flavor. He couldn't decide which one he liked best.

Jim took a bite of his bar. *Mmm!* Martian Mocha Chip!

Jim even liked the ads on TV.

There was always the same astronaut
doing a spacewalk. He would say, "Blast Off
Energy Bars—they're out of this world!"

One day Jim was munching on a Cosmic Cocoa Blast Off Bar. Something on the wrapper caught his eye.

No way! A trip to space camp? Just for saving a few wrappers?

Then he checked the fine print:

You need just 10,000 wrappers to win!

Even in tiny print, that was one big number—an impossible number.

Wasn't it?

Collect BLAST OFF BAR wrappers and win a at SPACE CAMP!

You need just 10,000 wrappers to win!

That night Jim dreamed he was wearing
a space suit and floating in zero gravity. He
was holding a Blast Off Bar—freeze-dried for
space. And he was saying, "Blast Off Bars—
they're out of this world!"

At breakfast, Jim had a Stellar Strawberry Blast Off Bar. When he was finished, he smoothed out the empty wrapper. Then he tucked it into his backpack.

He did the same thing at lunch that day, and every day that week.

Jim counted his wrappers on Friday.
"Only ten?" he moaned to Everett.
Jim wasn't sure how many more he
needed. But he knew it was a *lot*.

From then on, Everett gave all his Blast Off wrappers to Jim. So did Rachel.

On Tuesday, one of the fourth graders stopped by. "Are you the Blast Off Kid?" she asked.

"I guess I am," Jim replied.

She handed him the wrappers from her lunch table.

"Thanks!" said Jim. "News travels fast."

By Friday, Jim's backpack was stuffed with wrappers. He didn't even know how many he had. Each time he counted, he got a different number.

"I know," Jim said. "I'll use paper clips to put the wrappers in bundles of ten. Then it will be easy to see how many I have."

Tens	Ones
1	3

There was an assembly on Monday. The principal talked about school safety. Then two kids made announcements. That gave Jim an idea. He scribbled a note and brought it up to the principal.

"Students, one last thing," the principal said. "Please don't throw away your Blast Off Bar wrappers. Jim is collecting them."

A ripple of chatter went through the crowd. Jim heard a girl say, "Blast Off Kid" and laugh. Ugh. He felt embarrassed.

13

But it was worth it. By the end of lunch
that day, Jim's backpack was stuffed with
wrappers.

It happened again the next day . . .
and the day after that.

On Friday, Rachel and Everett helped
Jim count the bundles of wrappers. "I keep
losing my place," Everett said.

"Me, too," said Rachel.

"Wait!" Jim said. "I'll get some paper
bags. We can put ten bundles in each bag."

Soon they had filled up four bags. Each bag held 100 wrappers. There were two bundles and five loose wrappers left over.

"425 wrappers!" said Rachel.

"Wow!" said Everett. "Your announcement sure did the trick."

Everett is right, thought Jim. It's all about advertising. I've got to spread the word.

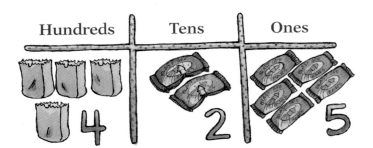

Hundreds	Tens	Ones
4	2	5

And that weekend, he did. He made some flyers. He put one up at the grocery store and left a collection box there. He did the same thing at the Internet Café, the video store, and the health club.

A week later, a woman from the health club called Jim. "Could you please come soon to pick up your wrappers?" she asked. "They're sort of taking over the front desk."

BLAST OFF WRAPPERS

SUPER·FIT ☆ CLASS ☆ SIGN UP!

Jim knew the feeling. The wrappers
were taking over his room, too.

"Jim," his mother called. She poked
her head in the door. "Are you in here?"

"Yeah, Mom," Jim said. His voice
came from somewhere behind the bed.

Jim and his mom carried his wrapper collection to the garage. They got trash bags and put ten grocery bags in each one. When they were done, they had filled six trash bags.

They also had three grocery bags, five bundles and four loose wrappers.

"That's 6,354 wrappers!" Jim said.

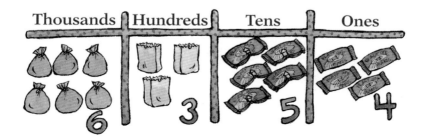

Thousands	Hundreds	Tens	Ones
6	3	5	4

Saturday afternoon a newspaper reporter rang the doorbell. "Are you Jim, the Blast Off Kid?" she asked. "I saw your flyers all over town."

The next morning, Jim opened the newspaper . . .

And there he was!

Before long, Jim started getting mail.
Only six envelopes came the first day.
But the next day there were twelve.

The following week, the mail carrier made
a special trip to Jim's house. His truck was
filled with wrappers for the Blast
Off Kid!

23

On Wednesday, Jim's dad was leaving for work. "Has anyone seen the car keys?" he asked. Jim's mom found them in the kitchen.

"Thanks," said Jim's dad. He opened the door to the garage. "Um . . . has anyone seen the car?" he asked.

"How many wrappers are in here, anyway?"
Jim's dad went on. They uncovered the car and
started counting.

There were nine trash bags, nine grocery
bags, nine bundles, and nine loose wrappers.
Jim gasped. "That means . . ."

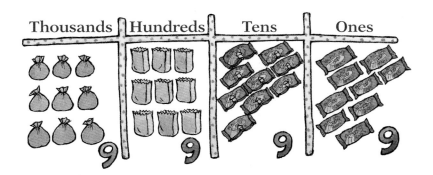

Thousands	Hundreds	Tens	Ones
9	9	9	9

Jim ran inside. He got a Galactic Grape Blast Off Bar and tore it open.

He added the wrapper to the nine loose wrappers. That was enough to make a bundle. Now he had ten bundles.

He put them into a grocery bag. Now he had ten grocery bags. He put them into a trash bag. Now he had ten trash bags!

"I have 10,000 wrappers!" Jim shouted.

Jim's mom called the Blast Off Energy Bar company. A month later, Jim was at space camp!

He wrote a postcard home. *Dear Mom and Dad,* he wrote, *I'm having a blast at space camp....*

Today I learned about rockets.

Yesterday I tried a flight simulator.

Tomorrow I'll ride in the low-gravity chair.

Oh, yeah! And I found out that I get a ton of Blast Off Bars to take home. I think I'll share them with everyone who helped me win! Love, Jim

P.S. Please don't throw away any Blast Off Energy Drink bottle caps. I heard they are starting a new contest.

PLACE VALUE CHART

Make counting easy. Group by ten!

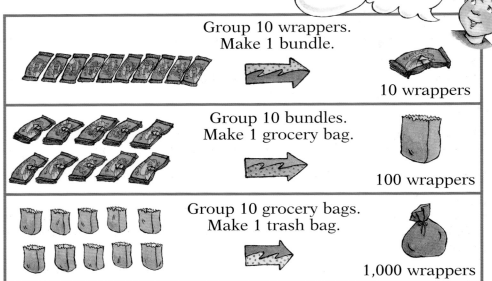

Group 10 wrappers. Make 1 bundle.

10 wrappers

Group 10 bundles. Make 1 grocery bag.

100 wrappers

Group 10 grocery bags. Make 1 trash bag.

1,000 wrappers

Charts help you read and write numbers.

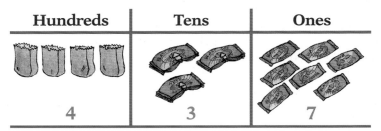

Hundreds	Tens	Ones
4	3	7

four hundred thirty-seven

Thousands	Hundreds	Tens	Ones
2	1	5	6

two thousand, one hundred fifty-six